be returned on or before
below.

ROMULUS AND REMUS

STOLEN WIVES

For Sophie

ORCHARD BOOKS
96 Leonard Street, London EC2A 4XD
Orchard Books Australia
14 Mars Road, Lane Cove, NSW 2066
This text was first published in Great Britain in the form of
a gift collection called *The Orchard Book of Roman Myths*,
illustrated by Emma Chichester Clark in 1999.
This edition first published in hardback in Great Britain in 2000
First paperback publication 2001
Text © Geraldine McCaughrean 1999
Illustrations © Tony Ross 2000
The rights of Geraldine McCaughrean to be identified as the author and
Tony Ross as the illustrator of this work have been asserted by them in
accordance with the Copyright, Designs, and Patents Act, 1988.
ISBN 1 84121 885 5 (hardback)
ISBN 1 84121 522 8 (paperback)
1 3 5 7 9 10 8 6 4 2 (hardback)
1 3 5 7 9 10 8 6 4 2 (paperback)
A CIP catalogue record for this book is available
from the British Library.
Printed in Great Britain

ROMULUS AND REMUS
STOLEN WIVES

GERALDINE MCCAUGHREAN
ILLUSTRATED BY TONY ROSS

ORCHARD BOOKS

ROMULUS AND REMUS

Empires rise and fall. The gods, who can see the future, know these things. That is why the gods of Greece gradually shifted ground to the skies over Italy. They came to be known by different names: not Zeus but Jupiter; not Hera but Juno; not winged Hermes but winged Mercury.

Around the shrine to Vesta a great temple was built, its 'vestal' priestesses the unmarried daughters of good families. Because all their love was promised to the goddess, they were forbidden, on pain of death, to give any love to a man.

Rhea Silvia did not: mortal men she could easily have resisted. But the god Mars – quarrelsome Mars, warrior-wild and handsome as only an immortal can be – wooed Rhea Silvia like war besieging a town. He blasted her with love, bombarded her with tender words, shot her full of passion. She could no more resist him than the flowers on the altar could resist the flames which ate them.

Finding she was pregnant, she tried to
hide her secret, but soon her slim figure
grew as round as a sail, and the other
priestesses whispered behind their hands,
"What is to be done? Rhea Silvia has
broken her vows! Rhea Silvia is giving
birth…to twins! Rhea Silvia must die!"

Her mother and father were important citizens – descendants of Aeneas himself. They might have pleaded for the life of their daughter or spirited her away to safety. Instead they upended their hearts and emptied out every last drop of love they had ever felt for her. "Bury her alive, as the law demands," they said. "Rhea Silvia must die!"

"But the babies? The twin boys! What will become of them?"

"Throw them into the River Tiber! The pity is that they were ever born!"

Brick by brick, Rhea Silvia was sealed

up in her tomb, those last bricks shutting out the sounds and sunlight of the living world. Mars could have shattered her prison with a single breath, but he had long since left Latium to batter some other lady's heart or to raise up war in the world.

As for the twin boys – Romulus and Remus – they were carried naked in a basket to the banks of the Tiber. The servants sent to carry out the task would have tipped them in, midstream. But the Tiber was in flood and the waters milled by with such terrifying force that they set the basket down on the muddy shore and watched till the swollen river swirled the children away towards a watery death.

Ah, but weren't Romulus and Remus the sons of Mars, the descendants of Aeneas? Though their tiny pink fists and feet were powerless to save them, they were strong, healthy boys. The cold did not kill them, nor the river spill them, nor pike snatch them down to a muddy death.

The basket was swept helter-skelter downstream until it snagged on tree roots and spun into a backwater where the wild creatures came to drink. A face loomed over the crying boys – a mask with yellow eyes and a mouth full of ravenous teeth.

The wolf opened wide her grinny jaws, seized on first Romulus, then Remus, and ran with them to her lair. There she dropped them among the soft, tumbling fur of her hungry cubs…

And there she suckled them, letting them drink, as her cubs drank, from her soft, warm underbelly. A woodpecker perched on a branch nearby to keep watch for danger. (If this seems strange past belief, you should know that wolf and woodpecker are creatures sacred to Mars.)

A herdsman found them. Out one day
hunting the wolves who threatened his
livestock, he found two big, squalling baby
boys, pink and brawling in a wolf-den,
and took them home.

Now the herdsman was no fool: he knew full well who they were – knew that the law had demanded their death. But he and his wife had no children of their own, and neither civic duty nor fear of punishment counted for anything alongside the joy those children brought them.

Perhaps Romulus and Remus drank down the ferocious courage of the she-wolf as they drank her milk. Perhaps they learned courage and endurance from her as she came and went, feeding and fighting for her young. Or perhaps, as sons of Mars, there was already warrior blood in their veins. But Romulus and Remus grew up into brave, quarrelsome boys who never shunned a fight and who never lost one either.

No shepherd life for them! No life in peaceful Latium. Even before their father told them the story of their birth, they were roaring boys, with roaring friends, their sights pinned on glory. They set their hearts on building a new city, a grand city, a city to rival Troy or Carthage or Athens.

"It shall be called Reme," said Remus.

"Rome, you mean," Romulus corrected him. They quarrelled about it, naturally; it was their way to squabble and row. Brothers do.

But where was their magnificent city to be built?

"Here," said Romulus, "where the she-wolf suckled us!"

"That's not where she suckled us," said Remus with a scornful snort. "It was over there, near that clump of trees."

"Never!" They squabbled and rowed. Brothers do. The gods looked on with mild amusement.

"Let the gods decide!" said Romulus.

"Yes, we'll watch for a sign," agreed Remus. The gods, too, nodded in agreement, and Jupiter sent

a flock of ravens to mark the spot fixed by
Destiny for the building of the sacred city.

"There! There! Look, three ravens!"
cried Remus. "The sacred birds of Jupiter!"

An acorn dropped from the claw of one bird and fell to earth. The brothers, however, were too busy arguing to notice where it fell.

"Seven ravens. There were seven not three," said Romulus.

"What does it matter? I saw them first. So I choose where Reme is built."

"But I saw more ravens than you!" protested Romulus. "So I shall build in my chosen place. You can do as you like…and it will be Rome, not Reme!" They exchanged a string of insults. Brothers do. The gods frowned a little at their squabbling. Time was going to waste.

Obstinate Romulus began to build – where the Tiber snaked between seven hills, where the sunbeams were blade-sharp and golden, and where the stones were mossy massive – heaping the boulders into a wall.

"Call that a wall?" jeered Remus.
"I've seen bigger pigsties!" and he jumped
over the low walling, his feet dislodging
pebbles, his taunts loud and sneering.

To and fro he jumped, deriding
Romulus's work until all brotherly
affection dissolved
in Romulus and
he hated his
brother with
a hot loathing.
Brothers can.
He picked
up a boulder.
"You do
that once
more…"

Remus jumped the wall. A whole section slumped down in a landslide of rocks and pebbles. Romulus lifted the boulder and brought it down on his brother's head. Remus was dead before he even hit the ground.

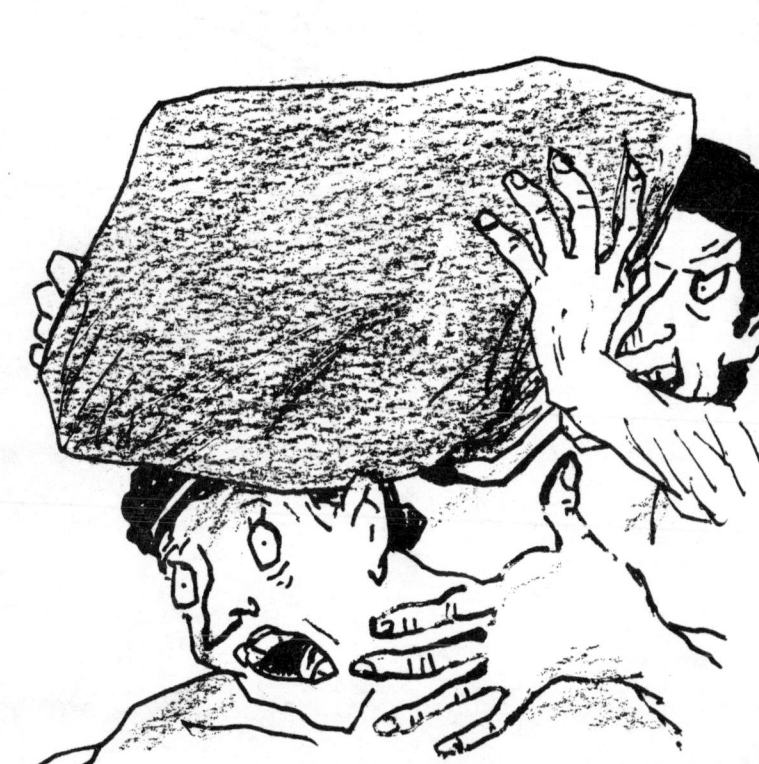

"Thus die all those who ever try to leap the walls of Rome!" Romulus crowed, as his young warrior friends ran to the spot and crowded round.

Then Romulus wept, because he had killed his best friend in the world, and all for the sake of a pile of stones.

The gods looked on with distaste. How could the destiny of an empire rest on the shoulders of such men?

"It is good," said Mars, dry-eyed, stony-faced. "It is good that blood should water the foundations of Rome."

But Jupiter shook his head. "They were fools to quarrel," he said.

"Their foolishness does not stop there," said Venus softly. "Look at them. An army of men building a city for themselves. How can there be a city without women? Where do they hope to find sons and daughters – floating on the Tiber or crying among the wolves?"

STOLEN WIVES

It was not long before the men of Rome noticed the lack of women. Though the city was finished (and it was very fine), there was no one in it to bake them bread or wash their shirts, nobody to tell them they were brave or handsome or wonderful.

"I have the answer," said Romulus. "Are we not warriors? Do we not have the cunning of Aeneas and the strength of Mars? We shall take wives enough for every house in Rome!"

He invited the neighbouring tribe to visit the gleaming new city of Rome – to join in the celebrations at its completion.

The Sabines were handsome people,
their womenfolk tall and red-haired and
beautiful. Once the visitors were sat down
to dine, their weapons stacked by the
door, their reflexes slow from drinking,

the Romans swept in like a whirlwind and
snatched the women up by the hair, by the
wrists, by the waist, carrying them off to
the safety of locked rooms. The men and
boys were driven out of the city like leaves

in front of a broom, and before they could gather their wits, found themselves sitting outside the gates, robbed of their daughters, sisters and wives.

No tears, no pleas, no prayers, no offers of ransom or threats of revenge – "Our men will never rest till they have us back!" – softened the hearts of the Roman men. They were too busy choosing themselves wives.

"That one in the grey."

"The fat one for me!"

"The one with the green eyes."

They were like children at a pet shop choosing rabbits or kittens.

Married against their will, the Sabine women found themselves keeping house,

singing songs,

tending wounds,

baking bread

and warming the beds of Roman husbands. They swore never to forgive their captors, to hate them for ever.

But of course hatred is as hard to keep alight as a hearth fire. The Roman men were not monsters; in most respects, they were just like Sabine men.

Some were handsome,

some funny,

some athletic, some artistic.

Some liked to dip their olive bread in their wine; some were afraid of spiders.

Not a day passed but the Sabine wives remembered their Sabine homes and husbands and the children lost to them. And yet this new life had its merits.

Babies were born – babies with Roman noses and Sabine hair – and their fathers doted on them and carved them little wooden boats to float on the Tiber. Romans made good fathers and honourable husbands. Now and then, their Sabine wives had to admit as much.

Then one day the Sabines came back.

Of course they came. Did Romulus really suppose that they could live without women any more than the Romans could? Did he really suppose the Sabines would rest until they had recaptured their wives, their mothers, their daughters?

From Rome's high walls, the Sabine army was sighted by the look-outs.

The great doors of the temple of Janus (which stand open in times of war) swung ajar like a mouth gaping, and the men scrambled to arm themselves for battle.

"Never fear, wives!" yelled the Sabine warriors from outside the walls. "We have come to rescue you, and we shall not rest till every Roman lies awash in his own blood!"

"Never fear," said the Romans to their wives as they whetted the swords and took up their battle shields. "We shall be victorious by sunset!"

The women did not reply except to pull their scarves over their faces and rock silently to and fro. They drifted together into the forum – women torn in two by divided loyalties.

At last, lifting up their small fry, cradling their babies, they broke into a run. Out of the city gates they ran, to where the Roman army was drawn up in battle lines before the massed ranks of the Sabines.

"Stop! Stop! Enough!" they shouted, holding up babies and children shoulder high. Baby clouts flapped whitely like flags of surrender. "Are we bones that you fight over us like dogs? Stop! Are we to see our husbands slaughtered by our brothers, our sons killed by our own fathers? Stop! Which of you could win a victory without breaking our hearts by it? Which of you could win today without winning our hatred? If women ruled, there would be

no war, for women are always the losers in any battle. Well, then! If you must fight, you must cut your way through us first, and through your little children! Better for us to die than that you hack our hearts in pieces!"

The jogging run of both advancing armies slowed to a halt. They glared at one another between the upraised arms of their women.

They craved the glory of battle; they loved fighting. But the women stood their ground, the children watching with big, terrified eyes. A silence fell, broken only by the crying of babies.

And the watching gods smiled at the men's predicament. At least Venus smiled and tucked a daisy behind the ear of Mars as the god of war watched helpless, gnashing his teeth with frustration. For the Romans and Sabines were striking a truce – surly and grudging, it's true, but a truce even so. There would be no war.

The women had won their way, and for a brief time at least, the doors of the temple of Janus swung closed again to declare a time of peace.